THE BOY WHO WANTED

BY SAM KIDD

Illustrated by Bijan Samaddar

THE BOY WHO WANTED TO DANCE

There once was a boy, who wanted to dance,
but his arms and legs, just didn't have, stance

He thought long and hard, and deep from within,
deciding to explore to let the learning begin

In the woods, he saw a bee keeper sing,
moving his legs, they both did swing

"Hey Mr, Sir, oh won't you help me,
to dance, and to move, to music, like thee”

“Yes, young lad, the moves of course!
Just twist your hips, with little to no force”

“Side to side, let them sway,
give it a go, and you'll be on your way!”

With that in mind, the boy did try,
and swinging his hips from side to side

"There you are, Look at you go!
You're dancing already, you look like a pro"

"But sir, your arms, they are not still!
Please show me how, to add to my skill"

"That my boy, is easy to share,
all you have to do, is put your hands in the air"

“Wave them too, from side to side,
and dance, dance, with glee and pride"

Later that day, and a farewell glance,
home he went, the boy who could dance.

THE BOY WHO WANTED TO DRIVE

There once was a boy, who wanted to drive,
out on the race track he dreamed he would thrive

He thought long and hard, and deep from within,
deciding to explore and let the learning begin

Down at the race track, the young boy went.
Watching the race cars, was time well spent

Then through the fence, the boy did see,
A race driver shouting, “Come race with me!”

Into the pits, and strapped to a seat
“You do the steering, and I’ll do the feet”

On the starting line now, the 4 wheeled machine
grumbling and watching for red to turn green.

42

Zoom! They were off with a puff of smoke.
The boy at the wheel and this racing car bloke.

Into the corners, and out on the straights,
round the bends and through the gates.

"You're doing great my lad", the driver said
"Now get ready to turn to the left up ahead"

Fast and then slow, left and then right,
the brakes were glowing, a brilliant bright white

Woosh they went, as they passed the crowd,
crossing the finish line, feeling very proud

"A dream come true", the young boy exclaimed!
"Come back tomorrow, we'll do more of the same"

A shake of the hands, and a big high five.
Home he went, the boy who could drive.

42

THE BOY WHO WANTED TO FLY

There once was a boy, who wanted to fly,
he dreamed of zooming around in the sky

He thought long and hard, and deep from within,
deciding to explore to let the learning begin

Down at the airport, a pilot was there,
he had boots, a jacket and oil in his hair

"Hey Mr, Sir, oh won't you help me,
to learn to fly would make me so happy”

“Yes, young lad, get over here!
Climb aboard, there’s nothing to fear”

The propeller swung round, and the engine fired,
this was everything the boy desired

Open the Throttle, and ready to soar.
The aircraft paced, and the engine roared

Up up, up and away,
this was already the greatest of days

The pilot gave the boy control
and showed him a loop, and then a roll

Upside down, and the right way up,
If you're having fun, give a big thumbs up!

Through the clouds they came back down
and landed so softly, back on the ground

"I've never from a lesson, had such fun",
said the boy to the pilot, with a setting sun

A short while later, and a pleasant good-bye.
Home he went, the boy who could fly.

THE BOY WHO WANTED TO FARM

There once was a boy, who wanted to farm,
to raise cute sheep, and turn their wool into yarn

To turn the fields by pulling a plough,
or collect sweet milk, straight from the cow

He thought long and hard and, deep from within,
deciding to explore and let the learning begin

Up to the farm, the young boy went
the air giving off that true farm scent

By the tractor a farmer stood,
wellies, a stick, and a big blue hood

"Oh Mr, Sir, won't you help me,
I want to be a farmer, and feel so free!"

“Yes my lad”, said the farmer with a smirk.
“But don’t be fooled, farming is very hard work”

They ploughed the fields, and milked the cows,
fed the goats, and tended the sows

Barky the sheepdog, came with a leap,
because next it was time, to round up the sheep

Now to harvest, the seasons crop,
and get them all ready to be sold in the shop

“Thank you sir, for letting me see,
the life of a farmer, might be for me!”

“You’re welcome my boy, you worked very hard.
You’re free anytime to come back to the yard”

A bag of carrots were thrown over his arm.
Home he went, the boy who could Farm.

THE BOY WHO WANTED TO PAINT

There once was a boy, who wanted to paint,
with the brush, paper, and colour to acquaint

He thought long and hard, and deep from within,
deciding to explore to let the learning begin

Up on the hill, he saw her there,
an artist, painting a big brown bear

“Hey Miss, Madam, won’t you help me,
to put to paper the world that you see”

A gentle smile and a tilt of the head
put down her brush and then she said

“Get over here and put on this gown,
and copy me as we paint the bear brown”

“Using green we paint all of the trees,
and when it's dry, we’ll add the leaves”

“Black small V’s make the birds fly,
and using blue to paint the sky”

She said to the boy “let this all be a lesson”
“With everything in life, be curious and question”

“Patience and care is worth the wait
for the power of the brush, lets us create”

The boy smiled with the wind in his hair,
and looked at his painting, of the big brown bear

They traded pictures, before it got too late.
Home he went, the boy who could paint.

THE BOY WHO WANTED TO COOK

There once was a boy, who wanted to cook,
with a big Chefs hat to complete the look

He thought long and hard, and deep from within,
deciding to explore to let the learning begin

From pan fried steak, to lemon tart.
The boy just didn't know where to start

In the restaurant, down at the inn
the boy saw a chef with a welcoming grin

"Hey Mr, Sir! Oh won't you help me.
Teach me to cook meals that make people happy"

He looked the boy up, then down,
And said "Into the kitchen, let me show you around".

Busy in the kitchen were lot of white shirts.
Sauces, entrées, mains and deserts.

“You see my young friend”, by a pan with steam,
“To make amazing food is all about the team”

“Here, take this knife, and dice up the meat,
and I’ll get to work on this yummy sweet treat”

Onto the plate, then the finishing touch,
a swirl of sauce but “Careful! Not too much”.

“Presentation, plus taste, can equal the world.
Look how happy your food made that girl”

At the end of the shift, the chefs hand he shook,
Home he went, the boy who could cook.

Printed in Great Britain
by Amazon